THE TROJAN HORSE
THE FALL OF TROY

A GREEK MYTH

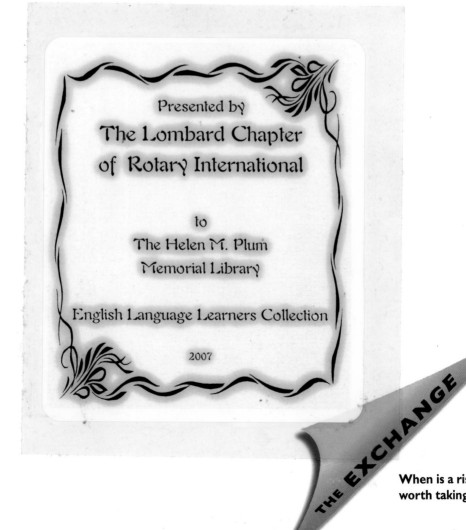

THE EXCHANGE

When is a risk
worth taking?

THE TROJAN HORSE
THE FALL OF TROY

A GREEK MYTH

JUSTINE & RON FONTES • GORDON PURCELL

 HAMPTON-BROWN

The Trojan Horse by Justine & Ron Fontes, illustrated by Gordon Purcell. Copyright © 2007 by Millbrook Press,
a division of Lerner Publishing Group. This edition is published by Hampton-Brown Company, Inc., by arrangement with
Graphic Universe, an imprint of Lerner Publishing Group, 241 First Avenue North, Minneapolis, MN 55401 U. S. A.

Hampton-Brown
P.O. Box 223220
Carmel, California 93922
800-333-3510
www.hampton-brown.com

Printed in the United States of America

ISBN-13: 978-0-7362-3156-5
ISBN-10: 0-7362-3156-0

06 07 08 09 10 11 12 13 14 15 10 9 8 7 6 5 4 3 2 1

TABLE OF CONTENTS

INTRODUCTION . . . 9

A ROTTEN APPLE . . . 13

THE WEARY WAR . . . 19

A WOEFUL WARNING . . . 29

THE SLEEPING CITY . . . 34

THE TOWERS TUMBLE . . . 44

GLOSSARY AND PRONUNCIATION GUIDE . . . 52

INDEX . . . 53

STORY BY
JUSTINE & RON FONTES

PENCILS BY
GORDON PURCELL

INKS BY
BARBARA SCHULZ

ADAPTED FROM VIRGIL'S *AENEID*
AND *THE WAR AT TROY*
BY QUINTUS OF SMYRNA

MOUNT
OLYMPUS

A E G E A N

GREECE

ITHACA

THEBES

MYCENAE

ATHENS

SPARTA

N

THE TROJAN HORSE

THE FALL OF TROY

A GREEK LEGEND

TENEDOS   TROY

TURKEY

INTRODUCTION

*T*he *Trojan Horse: The Fall of Troy* was inspired by an ancient Greek myth. This myth tells the story of a great war between the Greeks and the Trojans. No one is sure if the story was created or if it was based on an actual war that took place more than 3,000 years ago. What is known is that the ancient Greeks passed down the story of the Trojan War through many generations. Over time, the events and heroic deeds changed depending on the storyteller. Today, it is considered a popular legend of Greek **mythology** .

Scholars disagree about who was the first to write down the story. The Trojan War appeared in the writings of several ancient poets and philosophers. A blind poet named Homer may have been the first to write about it around 2,800 years ago in *The Iliad*. Homer's *The Iliad* describes the tenth year of that war. It does not reveal how the war ended. Writers later continued the story of *The Iliad*. They often tried to use Homer's storytelling style.

Very little is known about Homer. Scholars often wonder if he actually existed. Homer may have also written another famous Greek adventure, *The Odyssey*. It tells the story of what happens to the hero Odysseus after the Trojan War. Some scholars believe that several poets wrote *The Iliad* and *The Odyssey*. Regardless of who wrote *The Iliad*, it is the earliest record of the events surrounding the Trojan War that exists.

Key Concepts

mythology *n.* collection of ancient Greek myths about gods, goddesses, and heroes

According to the myth, the Trojan War begins because of a Greek woman named Helen. She is the daughter of the king of gods, Zeus, and the most beautiful woman in the world. Many men in Greece want to marry her. Helen's father must be **cautious**. He needs to choose a husband for Helen and he does not want to start a fight.

But the **consequences** of his decision may be terrible. Those who are not chosen might become angry. They might fight for her. They could even start a war. All the men make an agreement to make sure this will not happen. They all agree to protect Helen and whoever becomes her husband. Helen finally marries Menelaus. He will later become the king of Sparta. The other men accept the decision.

But everything does not go according to plan. After she is married, Helen falls in love with a Trojan named Paris. They run away from Greece, across the sea to the city of Troy. Helen's **betrayal** makes Menelaus angry. He makes the Greeks keep their promise to protect him and his wife. They must attack Troy. A war begins.

The Trojan Horse is a graphic novel about the Trojan War. In this retelling, the Greeks must make a choice. The war has to stop. Greek soldiers create a dangerous plan. Will their **strategy** work?

Key Concepts

cautious *adj.* careful

consequence *n.* result of a decision or action

betrayal *n.* disloyalty; the act of lying or helping an enemy

strategy *n.* plan to win or succeed at something

A ROTTEN APPLE

HISTORY IS FULL OF WARS. BUT ONE WAR WILL NEVER BE FORGOTTEN. OVER THREE THOUSAND YEARS AGO, THE GREEKS GATHERED THE *GREATEST* ARMY THE WORLD HAD EVER SEEN. ONE THOUSAND SHIPS SAILED TO TAKE THE MIGHTY CITY OF TROY. FOR TEN YEARS, THE BEST WARRIORS WAGED FIERCE BATTLE. BUT TROY'S TALL WALLS STILL STOOD. WHY WERE THEY FIGHTING? THE *TROUBLE STARTED WITH A WEDDING!*

WAGED FIERCE BATTLE fought in a difficult war

TROY'S TALL WALLS STILL STOOD the Greeks could not defeat the people of Troy

TROUBLE STARTED WITH war began because of

LONG AGO, THE GREEKS BELIEVED IN MANY GODS AND GODDESSES WHO RULED EVERYTHING FROM LOVE TO WAR. PEOPLE PRAYED TO DIFFERENT GODS ACCORDING TO THEIR NEEDS. A FISHERMAN WOULD PRAY TO POSEIDON FOR A GOOD CATCH — AND TO APHRODITE FOR A PRETTY WIFE.

ZEUS

WISE MORTALS WORSHIP THE KING OF THE GODS

OR FEEL THE *FIRE* OF MY LIGHTNING BOLTS!

HERA

ALL WHO WANT FERTILE FIELDS AND *HAPPY* HOMES REMEMBER THE QUEEN OF THE GODS.

APOLLO

WITHOUT MY FIERY *CHARIOT*, THE SUN WOULD NOT RISE!

ARES

WARRIORS PRAY TO THE GOD OF WAR FOR *VICTORY*.

APHRODITE

JUST AS *LOVERS* PRAY TO ME, THE GODDESS OF LOVE.

ATHENA

THE GREEK CAPITAL OF *ATHENS* WAS NAMED FOR ME, THE GODDESS OF WISDOM.

POSEIDON

SAILORS PRAY TO ME, THE POWERFUL GOD OF THE SEA.

FOR A GOOD CATCH to help him catch fish

MORTALS men and women

CHARIOT carriage pulled by horses

ONE GREEK KING MADE A *BIG* MISTAKE. HE INVITED ALL THE GODS AND GODDESSES TO HIS WEDDING, *EXCEPT* ERIS, THE GODDESS OF QUARRELS AND STRIFE. SUDDENLY, AT THE HEIGHT OF THE FEASTING AND FUN, *ERIS APPEARED!*

HERE IS A WEDDING PRESENT FOR YOU!

HA! THIS SHOULD MAKE A *BEAUTIFUL BRAWL!*

LOOK, A *GOLDEN APPLE!*

IT'S FOR *ME.* YOU SEE? IT SAYS IT'S FOR THE *FAIREST.*

WHO SAYS YOU ARE THE *FAIREST?* AM I NOT THE QUEEN OF THE GODS?

Uh-oh! THIS MEANS *TROUBLE!*

WHO DO *YOU* THINK IS THE PRETTIEST?

I WOULDN'T *DARE* TO SAY!

IF YOU ASK *ME,* IT'S ATHENA.

WHO ASKED YOU?

AT THE HEIGHT during the middle

MAKE A BEAUTIFUL BRAWL start a big fight

FAIREST most beautiful

SOON THE APPLE ARGUMENT CAME DOWN TO THE THREE MOST POWERFUL GODDESSES. HERA, ATHENA, AND APHRODITE ASKED *ZEUS* TO DECIDE.

SURELY, HUSBAND, I AM THE FAIREST!

FATHER, DO I NOT *EXCEL* IN BOTH BEAUTY AND WISDOM?

BUT, DADDY, YOU *KNOW* I'M THE PRETTIEST!

SILENCE! WOULD YOU TURN THE KING OF THE GODS INTO A BEAUTY CONTEST JUDGE?

TAKE YOUR DISPUTE TO PARIS, IN THE COUNTRYSIDE NEAR TROY.

THOUGH A *MERE* MORTAL, THIS HANDSOME SHEPHERD IS AN *EXCELLENT* JUDGE OF BEAUTY.

A SHEPHERD?

I'LL HAVE THE SIMPLE *FOOL* EATING OUT OF MY HAND.

A *HANDSOME* SHEPHERD.

I'LL SOON HAVE PARIS WRAPPED AROUND MY LITTLE FINGER.

THANK YOU, FATHER. YOUR *WISDOM* IS EVEN GREATER THAN YOUR POWER.

WAY TO AVOID *TROUBLE,* OLD MAN. HERE'S HOPING THAT SHEPHERD IS AS WISE AS YOU!

EATING OUT OF MY HAND choosing me

WRAPPED AROUND MY LITTLE FINGER convinced
that I am the most beautiful

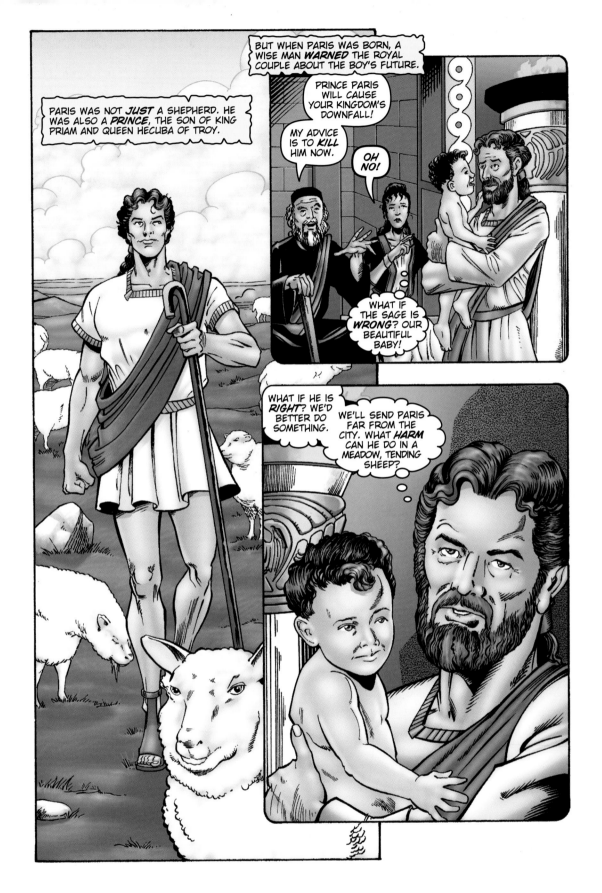

YOUR KINGDOM'S DOWNFALL Troy to be
destroyed

SAGE wise man

MEADOW, TENDING field, taking care of

SO THAT IS WHERE THE THREE GODDESSES FOUND PARIS.

YOU HAVE BEEN **CHOSEN** TO DECIDE WHICH OF US IS THE FAIREST.

IF YOU ARE **WISE**, YOU'LL GIVE THE GOLDEN APPLE TO ME.

WHAT A **HANDSOME** YOUNG MAN! I KNOW YOU'LL PICK ME.

THREE BEAUTIFUL GODDESSES IN MY PASTURE.

THIS SURE BEATS THE USUAL DUMB SHEEP!

CHOOSE ME AND I WILL GRANT YOU A **HAPPY** HOME.

CHOOSE ME AND GAIN **GLORY** AND **WISDOM**.

FATHER SURE WOULD BE **PROUD** OF ME IF I BECAME A GREAT GENERAL.

I CAN GIVE YOU THE MOST **BEAUTIFUL** WOMAN IN THE WORLD.

HER NAME IS **HELEN**.

WHO IS SHE? WHEN CAN I MEET HER?

SWAYED BY THE POWER OF **LOVE**, PARIS GAVE THE APPLE TO APHRODITE.

SHE **BRIBED** HIM!

YOU'RE JUST ANGRY BECAUSE PARIS DIDN'T ACCEPT YOUR BRIBE.

OR MINE, THE **FOOL**!

SURE BEATS is a lot better than

SWAYED Convinced, Persuaded

BRIBED HIM gave him something to choose her

BEFORE YOU MOVE ON...

1. **Conflict** What problem starts this story? Who is Paris, and how can he solve the problem?

2. **Summarize** Reread page 17. How is Paris a threat to Troy? What do his parents decide to do with him?

LOOK AHEAD Why will the Greeks declare war on Troy? Read pages 19–33 to find out.

THE WEARY WAR

APHRODITE SOON KEPT HER PROMISE. A POET DESCRIBED HELEN AS "MORE LOVELY THAN THE EVENING AIR CLAD IN THE BEAUTY OF A THOUSAND STARS."

SHE'S SO ... *BEAUTIFUL!*

UNFORTUNATELY, APHRODITE HAD *NOT MENTIONED* THAT HELEN WAS ALREADY MARRIED.

AND THIS IS MY *WIFE,* QUEEN HELEN.

WIFE?

APHRODITE USED HER POWERS TO PERSUADE HELEN TO SNEAK AWAY WITH PARIS.

I *KNOW* I SHOULDN'T BE DOING THIS, AND I FEAR MY ACTIONS WILL CAUSE TROUBLE.

BUT PARIS IS *SO HANDSOME* AND *EXCITING.*

NATURALLY, KING MENELAUS WAS *NOT* PLEASED. HE CALLED TOGETHER HIS MANY *POWERFUL* FRIENDS. THEY WERE LEADERS AND WARRIORS FROM ALL OVER GREECE, LIKE HIS BROTHER KING *AGAMEMNON,* THE GIANT *AJAX,* BRAVE *ACHILLES,* AND CLEVER *ODYSSEUS.*

I HAVE GATHERED YOU HERE TO REMIND YOU OF YOUR *PLEDGE* TO DEFEND HELEN AND WHOMEVER SHE CHOSE TO BE HER HUSBAND.

THAT SEEMED LIKE A *BETTER* IDEA WHEN I THOUGHT SHE'D MARRY ME.

TRAPPED BY MY OWN CLEVERNESS!

I PROPOSED THE PLEDGE SO GREECE WOULD NOT BE TORN APART BY ALL OF US WHO WANTED HELEN'S HAND.

AND NOW IT SEEMS WE MUST FIGHT OVER HELEN ANYWAY.

CLAD IN filled with

PLEDGE promise

HELEN'S HAND to marry Helen

THE GREEK HEROES HONORED THEIR PROMISE. THEY ASSEMBLED A HUGE FLEET TO FOLLOW HELEN AND PARIS ACROSS THE WINE-DARK SEA. THE SHIPS WERE FILLED WITH WEAPONS AND WARRIORS.

I'D RATHER BE *HOME* IN ITHACA WITH PENELOPE AND OUR SON. BUT EVEN I COULD NOT FIND A WAY OUT OF OUR PLEDGE.

THERE'S NOTHING LIKE A GOOD *WAR* FOR BUILDING UP MUSCLES!

YOUR *MUSCLES* ARE LARGE ENOUGH, MY FRIEND.

WAR IS MORE THAN EXERCISE, AJAX. IT IS A CHANCE TO GROW IN *POWER, RICHES,* AND *GLORY!*

MEANWHILE IN TROY, THE ROYAL FAMILY GREETED PARIS AND HELEN. EVERYONE WAS CHARMED BY HELEN'S BEAUTY—*EXCEPT PARIS'S SISTER, CASSANDRA.*

WELCOME, MY SON! THESE OLD EYES ARE GLAD TO SEE YOU. AND *DAZZLED* BY YOUR COMPANION'S BEAUTY!

WELCOME, PARIS! TO SEE YOU AGAIN BRINGS ME GREAT JOY.

PARIS BRINGS TROY'S DOOM!

IF YOU WILL NOT HEED MY WARNING, AT LEAST RECALL THE PROPHECY MADE AT HIS BIRTH.

DO NOT BE *LULLED* BY HER BEAUTY. THIS WOMAN WILL BE *THE DEATH OF TROY!*

PLEASE FORGIVE YOUR SISTER, PARIS. CASSANDRA IS EVER ONE TO SPEAK HER MIND.

TOO BAD SHE'S *COMPLETELY* MAD! I REALLY *MUST* MARRY HER OFF TO SOME DISTANT KING.

THE SUN GOD APOLLO HIMSELF HAD GRANTED CASSANDRA THE GIFT OF PROPHECY. IN EXCHANGE, SHE PROMISED HIM HER LOVE. THEN WHEN THE GIRL REFUSED THE GOD, APOLLO TURNED HER GIFT INTO A *CURSE.*

CASSANDRA! IS THAT ANY WAY TO SPEAK TO YOUR BROTHER AND HIS BELOVED?

O, CRUEL FATE! TO SEE THE *TRUTH,* TO SPEAK THE *TRUTH,* AND NEVER BE BELIEVED!

SO NO ONE HEEDED CASSANDRA'S WARNING. HELEN REMAINED IN TROY. AND IN TIME, HER HUSBAND'S HUGE ARMY ARRIVED.

HEED listen to

LULLED tricked, fooled

SPEAK HER MIND say what she thinks

THE ENORMOUS GREEK ARMY CAMPED ON THE PLAINS OUTSIDE THE WALLED CITY. FOR *TEN BLOODY YEARS*, THE GREEKS BATTLED THE TROJANS.

MANY MEN DIED *ON BOTH SIDES*, INCLUDING AJAX, ACHILLES, AND PARIS. KING PRIAM, QUEEN HECUBA, HELEN, AND THE REST OF TROY MOURNED THEIR LOSS.

I SHOULD HAVE KILLED HIM AS A BABE, BUT I HAD NOT THE HEART.

OH, PARIS, MY UNLUCKY SON!

OH, SWEET PARIS, HOW MANY MORE *WILL DIE* FOR OUR LOVE?

WILL THIS WAR NEVER END?

WE MUST FIND A WAY TO *AVENGE MY FATHER'S DEATH!* HIS SHADE *CRIES OUT FOR BLOOD!*

ACHILLES WAS NOT THE ONLY ONE TO DIE, NEOPTOLEMUS. MANY *BRAVE MEN* HAVE GONE TO HADES'S KINGDOM BENEATH THE EARTH. ODYSSEUS, THERE MUST BE *SOME WAY* TO WIN THIS ENDLESS WAR.

EVEN I AM TIRED OF FIGHTING.

I HAVE A PLAN THAT CAN END TEN YEARS OF WAR IN JUST THREE DAYS.

AS LONG AS WE AVENGE ACHILLES, MY SWORD IS READY.

WE WILL KILL THEM ALL!

GOOD! I'M SICK OF ARMY FOOD.

YOU GOT THAT RIGHT!

YOU TELL 'EM, AGAMEMNON!

HAD NOT THE HEART could not kill my child

SHADE CRIES OUT FOR BLOOD ghost wants revenge

GONE TO HADES'S KINGDOM BENEATH THE
EARTH been killed in battle

21

BARRACKS shelters

FORM A DETAIL TO INVESTIGATE. Gather soldiers
to see what has happened.

STAY SHARP Be ready for anything

YOUR OWN EYES what you see

WHAT IN THE NAME OF ZEUS IS THAT? What is that?

MASTERPIECE beautiful work of art

IS EVERYTHING GLOOM AND DOOM WITH YOU do you
think that everything will lead to disaster

THE DOG the cheat; the liar

BE MERCIFUL let you live

SACRIFICE TO THE GODS FOR A SAFE VOYAGE gift to
the gods to make sure the Greeks return home safely

GAIN THE GODDESS'S FAVOR FOR YOURSELVES convince
Athena to help the Trojans

GIVE HIM A CHANCE let him live

A WOEFUL WARNING

Just then, *Laocoön*, priest of Poseidon the sea god, ran through the city gates. His wife and sons followed. Laocoön could not believe the other Trojans trusted this strange Greek gift.

HAVE YOU ALL GONE MAD?

THE HORSE MUST BE A TRICK. I FEAR THE GREEKS, EVEN WHEN THEY BEAR GIFTS!

Laocoön threw his spear as hard as he could.

DESTROY THE EVIL THING, AND SAVE OUR CITY!

HACK IT TO PIECES!

THUNK!

HE'S *RIGHT!* THIS HORSE WILL BE *TROY'S DOOM!* PLEASE, YOU MUST LISTEN TO ME AND IF NOT TO ME, TO THE PRIEST OF POSEIDON.

BEAR give us

HACK chop

SERPENTS SLITHERED snakes came

BETTER HIM THAN ME! I am glad they are moving toward him instead of me!

THE TERRIFIED CROWD PARTED AS THE CREATURES SPED TOWARD LAOCOÖN AND HIS SONS. THEIR *FORKED TONGUES* FLICKED, AND THEIR *RED EYES* FLASHED.

WITH A HORRIBLE HISSING, THE SERPENTS SANK THEIR FANGS INTO THE BOYS AND CAPTURED THEM IN THEIR CRUSHING COILS.

HELP! DADDY!

HELP!

LAOCOÖN TRIED TO HELP BUT WAS SOON OVERPOWERED BY THE HIDEOUS CREATURES.

LET THEM GO, YOU FIENDS!

MY FAMILY! WON'T SOMEONE SAVE *MY FAMILY*?

HERA, HAVE MERCY!

IT'S THE WILL OF THE GODS FOR DEFILING THIS OFFERING!

SO THE PRIEST AND HIS SONS SANK BENEATH THE WAVES.

POSEIDON MUST HAVE SENT THE SERPENTS!

SANK THEIR FANGS INTO bit

FIENDS monsters

IT'S THE WILL OF THE GODS FOR DEFILING THIS OFFERING! The gods are angry because he attacked the horse!

THE TROJANS DECIDED
THE DEATH OF
LAOCOÖN MUST BE A
SIGN THAT ATHENA
WAS ANGRY AT THE
PRIEST FOR SPEARING
HER STATUE. THEY
QUICKLY WIDENED THE
CITY GATES AND PUT
THE HORSE ON
ROLLERS. THE
SURVIVING MEN OF
TROY GLADLY LENT
THEIR STRENGTH TO
PUSH IT THROUGH THE
WIDENED GATES INTO
THE MAIN SQUARE OF
THE CITY.

WE'LL
TAKE IT TO
ATHENA'S
TEMPLE!

SPEARING throwing his spear at

LENT THEIR STRENGTH TO helped

SQUARE section

FEAST huge meal

BEFORE YOU MOVE ON...

1. **Conclusions** Reread page 20. Why does no one believe Cassandra when she predicts that Paris will cause Troy to fall?

2. **Cause and Effect** Reread pages 31–33. The Trojans think Athena sent the snakes. What does this cause them to do? Why?

LOOK AHEAD Read pages 34–43 to find out if the horse really is a sacrifice to Athena.

PEACE HAD COME the war was over

OUR GOOD FORTUNE ending the war

BURST ran

DANCE AT celebrate

HAVE FIXED OUR FATE are going to help the Greeks kill us

35

**CONDUCT YOURSELF WITH A BIT MORE THOUGHT
TO YOUR ROYAL STATION** behave like a princess

FRUSTRATE FATE change the future

EXHAUSTED WITH JOY, FOOD, AND WINE, THE TROJANS SOON SLEPT SOUNDLY. INSTEAD OF SHARPLY STEPPING SENTRIES AND THE QUIET CLINK OF SHOULDERED SWORDS, THE NIGHT WAS FILLED WITH SNORES.

SLEEP *DEEP*, MY TRUSTING ENEMIES!

SHARPLY STEPPING SENTRIES AND THE QUIET CLINK OF SHOULDERED the sounds of marching soldiers carrying

DEEP well

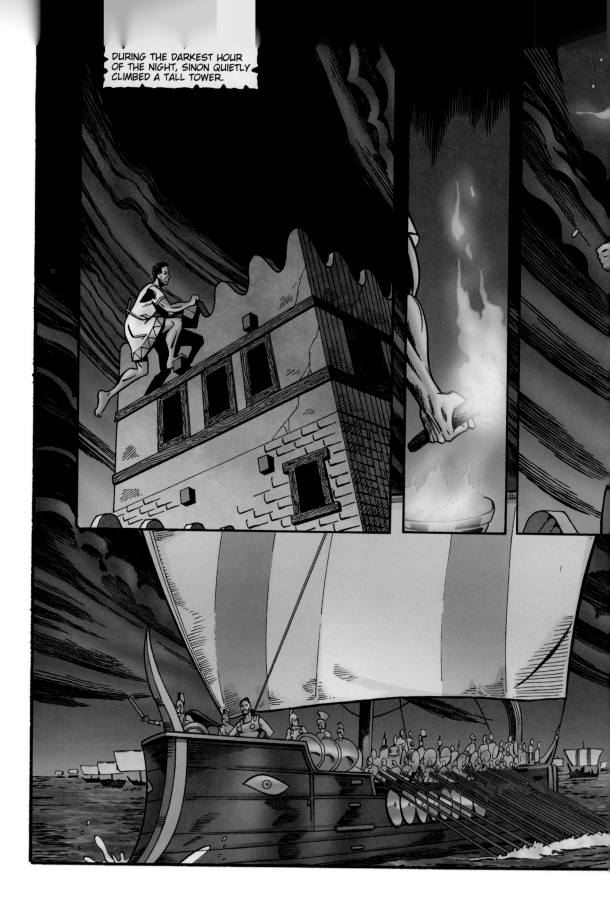

DURING THE DARKEST HOUR OF THE NIGHT, SINON QUIETLY CLIMBED A TALL TOWER.

SENTRY lookout, watchman

LIFTED ANCHORS, UNFURLED SAILS, AND SLAPPED
OARS INTO THE WATER prepared the ship to leave

MEANWHILE, SINON SNEAKED PAST SLEEPING TROJANS TO THE WOODEN HORSE.

HE OPENED A HATCH HIDDEN IN THE BEAST'S LEG. THE SMELL OF MANY MEN CONFINED IN CLOSE QUARTERS GREETED HIM.

IT'S *TIME!*

HATCH secret door

CONFINED IN CLOSE QUARTERS hiding in a small space

HORRIBLE ORDEAL terrible experience

EXCITEMENT RIPPLED THROUGH THE
DARKNESS. The soldiers were excited.

ALL WOULD BE LOST their plan would be ruined

SET FIRE TO burned

SLIT MANY SLEEPING THROATS killed many
sleeping soldiers

I MUST FIND PRIAM! THE KING MUST DIE!

BEFORE YOU MOVE ON...

1. **Plot** What is the real reason the Greeks give the horse to the Trojans?

2. **Sequence** The Greeks use Sinon to make sure the horse gets inside Troy. How does Sinon help the Greeks next?

LOOK AHEAD Will Odysseus's plan to defeat the Trojans work? Read pages 44–51 to find out.

THE TOWERS TUMBLE

THE FLAMES WERE ALREADY SPREADING BY THE TIME THE TROJANS WOKE. THEY SCRAMBLED FOR THEIR WEAPONS AND ARMOR.

GREEKS!

GET UP! AWAKE!

FIRE!!

TO ARMS! FIGHT FOR TROY!

WHAT'S HAPPENING?

HELP!!

ATHENA, HELP US!

ZEUS HAVE MERCY ON US!

MEANWHILE, IN THE PALACE, THE KING PREPARED TO DEFEND TROY.

MY CITY!

LEAVE THE FIGHTING TO THE *YOUNG MEN.*

YOU ARE TOO OLD, MY LOVE. COME TO THE ALTAR WITH ME. LET US PRAY.

AND, IF IT MUST BE, LET US AT LEAST *ALL DIE TOGETHER.*

SCRAMBLED FOR hurried to grab

TO ARMS! Get your weapons!

ALTAR place of religious worship

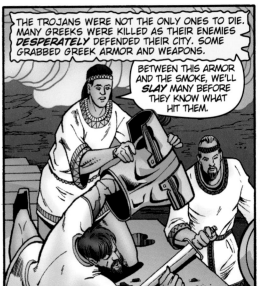

THE TROJANS WERE NOT THE ONLY ONES TO DIE. MANY GREEKS WERE KILLED AS THEIR ENEMIES *DESPERATELY* DEFENDED THEIR CITY. SOME GRABBED GREEK ARMOR AND WEAPONS.

BETWEEN THIS ARMOR AND THE SMOKE, WE'LL *SLAY* MANY BEFORE THEY KNOW WHAT HIT THEM.

ALTHOUGH GROGGY AND CONFUSED, THE TROJANS FOUGHT DESPERATELY TO SAVE THEIR CITY. BUT THEY FOUGHT IN VAIN.

FOR TROY!

O MIGHTY ZEUS! BRING US VICTORY IN OUR HOUR OF NEED!

ZEUS HEARS YOU NOT, MY NOBLE FATHER. *ALL IS LOST.*

I GUESS THIS ISN'T THE TIME FOR I-TOLD-YOU-SO'S, BUT I DID!

PREPARE TO *DIE*, OLD FOOL!

WHAT HIT THEM what is happening to them

FOUGHT IN VAIN could not win

I-TOLD-YOU-SO'S saying I told you to listen to me

HEAVE Push

BY ARES Thank goodness

ARE LOST will never survive

THEY TRICKED US!

LAOCOÖN WAS RIGHT! SO WAS CASSANDRA.

THE GODS HAVE DESERTED US!

HAVE DESERTED US will not save us

MAKE YOU PAY punish you

IS AVENGED now has his revenge

FORESIGHT OF ability to see the future like

THE MAIN BODY OF THE GREEK ARMY MARCHED THROUGH THE OPEN GATES. THE *GREAT CITY* OF TROY WAS SOON NOTHING MORE THAN BLOODY CORPSES AND CHARRED RUINS.

SPARE THE WOMEN AND CHILDREN! WE CAN *SELL THEM* AS SLAVES.

TROY'S WOMEN AND CHILDREN WERE TAKEN AWAY IN CHAINS.

BETTER A SLAVE THAN DEAD.

ARE YOU *SURE*?

THIS PRETTY *PRINCESS* IS QUITE A PRIZE!

BUT I MAY AS WELL *DIE* IN MYCENAE AS HERE. KNOWING THE FUTURE IS *NO GIFT* WHEN THE FUTURE IS SO DARK.

WHAT *TREASURE!*

WE'LL ALL BE *RICH!*

IF WE GET OUR FAIR SHARE.

WHEN MENELAUS FOUND HELEN, HE RAISED HIS SWORD TO STRIKE.

DIE, *FAITHLESS* WOMAN!

SPARE ME, *MY KING!*

THE MAIN BODY OF Many soldiers in

BLOODY CORPSES AND CHARRED RUINS dead
bodies and burning buildings

SPARE Do not kill

BUT HIS BROTHER STOPPED HIM.

THE GODS AND PARIS LED HER *ASTRAY*. WHO OF US CAN *RESIST* THE GODS?

THAT IS TRUE, MY BROTHER. SHE IS ONLY A *WOMAN*, AFTER ALL.

I NEVER MEANT TO *BETRAY* YOU.

AFTER ALL THIS, *I* LOVE HER STILL!

SO KING MENELAUS AND HIS QUEEN WERE REUNITED AT LAST. THEY SET SAIL OVER THE WINE-DARK SEA.

I *FORGIVE* YOU, HELEN.

IF IT IS POSSIBLE, YOU ARE EVEN MORE *BEAUTIFUL* THAN BEFORE.

THESE PAST TEN YEARS HAVE BEEN A *NIGHTMARE*. LET US HOPE OUR FUTURE TOGETHER WILL BE A *SWEET* DREAM.

I PRAY TO THE GODS THAT IT BE SO.

LED HER ASTRAY forced her to leave you

REUNITED back together

IT BE SO our lives will be happy

THE REMAINING GREEK SOLDIERS *FINALLY* HEADED FOR HOME TO THEIR FAMILIES, FRIENDS, FARMS, AND FIELDS. *OR SO THEY THOUGHT.*

I CAN HARDLY *BELIEVE* IT! SOON, I WILL HOLD MY *BELOVED WIFE* PENELOPE IN MY ARMS AGAIN.

SET SAIL, MEN, *FOR ITHACA AND HOME!*

YOU ARE NOT AS *CLEVER* AS YOU THINK, ODYSSEUS. YOU HAVE *ANGERED* THE GREAT POSEIDON.

IN YOUR *SELFISH PURSUIT* OF *GLORY*, YOU CAUSED THE DEATH OF MY GRANDSON, *PALAMEDES*.

SOON MY MIGHTY WAVES WILL TEACH YOU THAT *NO MORTAL DARE DEFY THE GODS!*

BUT BECAUSE OF POSEIDON'S CURSE, IT WOULD BE MANY LONG YEARS AND MANY MORE ADVENTURES BEFORE ODYSSEUS RETURNED TO ITHACA.

HEADED FOR went

IN YOUR SELFISH PURSUIT OF GLORY While you fought to win the war

MORTAL DARE DEFY human should ever anger

BEFORE YOU MOVE ON...

1. **Summarize** Reread pages 46–47. What is Odysseus's clever plan?

2. **Conclusions** Reread page 50. Why does Helen run away with Paris? Why does King Menelaus decide to take her back?

GLOSSARY AND PRONUNCIATION GUIDE

ACHILLES (uh-*kil*-eez): son of Peleus and Thetis; prince of Phthia and Greek hero

AGAMEMNON (a-ga-*mem*-non): king of Mycenae; high king of the Achaeans

AJAX (*ay*-jax): Greek hero

APHRODITE (a-fro-*dye*-tee): goddess of love

APOLLO (uh-*pol*-oh): god of prophesy, music, and healing

ARES (*air*-eez): the god of war

ATHENA (uh-*thee*-nuh): goddess of wisdom

CASSANDRA (kuh-*san*-druh): daughter of King Priam and Queen Hecuba

ERIS (*ee*-ris): the goddess of discord

HADES (*hay*-deez): god of the dead

HECUBA (*hek*-yoo-buh): wife of King Priam

HELEN (*hell*-en): wife of King Menelaus. She caused the Trojan War after fleeing with Paris.

HERA (*hehr*-ruh): queen of the gods; goddess of the hearth

LAOCOÖN (lay-*uh*-koh-uhn): priest of Poseidon. He was killed by serpents after he warned the city of Troy to destroy the Trojan horse.

MENELAUS (meh-neh-*lay*-uhs): king; brother of Agamemnon

NEOPTOLEMUS (nee-op-*to*-leh-muhs): son of Achilles

ODYSSEUS (o-*dis*-see-uhs): king of Ithaca

PALAMEDES (pa-luh-*mee*-deez): prince of Nauplia; cousin of Agamemnon

PARIS (*pa*-ris): son of King Priam and Queen Hecuba

PENELOPE (pe-*nel*-oh-pee): wife of Odysseus

POSEIDON (po-*seye*-duhn): god of the ocean and earthquakes

PRIAM (*preye*-am): king of Troy

SINON (*si*-non): Greek spy who deceived Troy into bringing the Trojan horse into the city

ZEUS (*zyoos*): king of the gods; god of thunder and sky

ink from pages 12–13

INDEX

Aphrodite 14, 15, 16, 18, 19

Athena 14, 15, 16, 18, 28, 32, 33, 46

Athens 14

Cassandra: prophecies of, 20, 26, 29, 35–36, 49; reactions to, 20, 36

gods and goddesses 14

Greek army 13, 20, 21, 39, 46, 49

Helen 18–21, 49, 50

Hera 14, 15, 16, 18

Ithaca 20, 51

Laocoön 28, 29, 31, 47

Menelaus 19, 42, 49, 50

Neoptolemus 21, 42, 48

Odysseus 19, 21, 42, 46, 51

Paris 16, 17–21, 50; prophecy about, 17

Poseidon: curse of, 51

serpents 30–31

Sinon 26, 27, 28, 37, 38–39, 40

Trojan horse 24–25, 26, 28, 29, 32–33, 34, 40–43

Trojans: celebration of, 34–35, 37

Trojan war: cause of, 13, 15–19; final battle of, 42–49; length of, 13, 21

Troy 13, 16, 17, 20, 33, 39, 44, 49